A Little Mo
of Peace j

. . . .

CW00867003

First published in Great Britain in 2018 by Hodder & Stoughton

An Hachette UK company

1

A CIP catalogue record for this title is available from the British Library

ISBN 978 1 473 69167 4
eBook ISBN 978 1 473 69168 1

Set in Baskerville by Anna Woodbine, thewoodbineworkshop.co.uk
Printed and bound in Italy by Lego S.p.A.

Hodder & Stoughton policy is to use papers that are natural, renewable and recyclable products and made from wood grown in sustainable forests. The logging and manufacturing processes are expected to conform to the environmental regulations of the country of origin.

Hodder & Stoughton Ltd
Carmelite House
50 Victoria Embankment
London EC4Y 0DZ

www.hodderfaith.com

Dear Parents

I have called these books Little Moments *(not* Vast Hours!*)
because I want them to be just that. A moment to pause in you and
your child's busy day. A moment to step away from the hustle and
bustle of life. A moment simply to be still.*

*The Bible is full of the most amazing stories, written down by many
authors over hundreds of years, all of them inspired to share the story
of this wonderful God and his amazing love for his children.
The words in this book are not literal translations – they are inspired
by verses and passages that I love.*

*My hope for all my readers, big and small, is that the
words and pictures will connect you to the true heart of God
and that the truth of who God is and how much
God loves you will nestle deep in your heart.*

Jenny

God, your peace is a

g i f t

that lies within the

pages of your love

story to me.

John 14:27

I've found a place
where I can be,
still and q u i e t,
just
you & me.

Psalm 46:10

You speak to the waves and they soften at the sound of your voice.

Psalm 107:29

You lift me up
and place me on a solid
rock where there is peace.

Psalm 40:2

Your peace
draws me into
your arms
of *love*.

The sweetness
of your peace
takes all my
fear away.

Psalm 119:103

I throw my worries up to heaven.

In return your words of
love speak to my heart.

1 Peter 5:7

God says,
'I have your hand in mine,
I'm holding onto you
and I will help you.'

Isaiah 41:13

Being kind will leave

a gift of peace

in someone's heart.

Ephesians 2:10

When we make peace with
our friends we will be
filled with joy.

Romans 12:18

Sow seeds

of peace and reap

a beautiful harvest.

James 3:18

Live in peace
with everyone and look
for ways to encourage
even a stranger.

Romans 14:19

The one who is gentle

will enjoy

a b u n d a n t

peace.

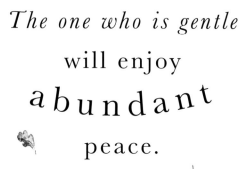

Psalm 37:11

God places you
in the palm of his hand,
where
you
are
safe.

God stoops down
to listen to me and
places my words in
his heart.

Psalm 116:2

When I think of you, God,
my heart is stilled.
I am at peace and
I *l e a n* into your love.

Take time to be
still.

Worry will steal away
your peace and keep
you from knowing
God's fullness.

Matthew 13:22

There's no need to worry
about anything!
Whisper all your concerns
straight to God...

Philippians 4:6

...who is
always listening
and loves to
answer you.

God's path of peace
leads me to a quiet meadow
and s t r e a m s
of life.

God's peace
is **bigger** than
all my thoughts and it
stands guard over my
heart
and
mind.

Philippians 4:7

Every single day
God carries our
burdens and never
grows tired.

Psalm 68:19

God's feathers of peace

f

a

l

l

from heaven to cover you.

Psalm 91:4

God your protector

will sit with you as you wait
for the storm to pass.

Psalm 5:11

Take time to listen
to God's voice
and heartbeat.
God will show
you the best way to go.

Proverbs 3:6

Peace

prepares

a path

for

your

s t e p s.

Proverbs 3:17

God has s t r e t c h e d
out your life like an
open book and made
a wonderful path
for you to follow.

Psalm 139

Don't be
afraid of
tomorrow
because you
are walking
with God.

God's angels watch over me
all through
the night, bringing
peace to my mind,
love to my heart and
safety to my body.

Psalm 121

Run from a house
of fear and
make peace
your home.

Isaiah 32:18